by Keith Yoder
illustrated by Wallace Keller

Printed in China

ISBN 10: 0-15-351504-X
ISBN 13: 978-0-15-351504-0

Ordering Options
ISBN 10: 0-15-351213-X (Grade 3 Advanced Collection)
ISBN 13: 978-0-15-351213-1 (Grade 3 Advanced Collection)
ISBN 10: 0-15-358094-1 (package of 5)
ISBN 13: 978-0-15-358094-9 (package of 5)

4 5 6 7 8 9 10 0940 12 11 10 09

Groundhog had lived on the farm for a long time. His father and mother had lived here, and their father and mother, and their father and mother before them. Years ago, Groundhog had moved into the barn.

Days were quiet now because the farmer had grown older and no longer farmed. Groundhog had dug his burrow in the barn for protection from the wind, and it remained dry and cozy in winter. He had built many tunnels under the barn and had a good, safe home.

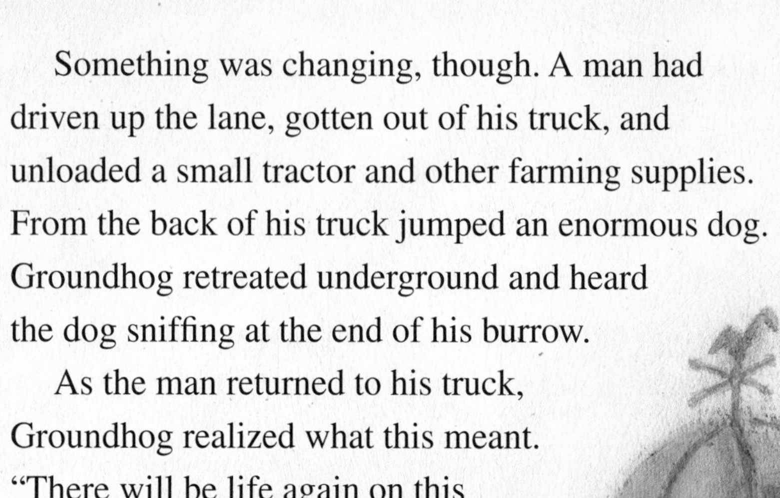

Something was changing, though. A man had driven up the lane, gotten out of his truck, and unloaded a small tractor and other farming supplies. From the back of his truck jumped an enormous dog. Groundhog retreated underground and heard the dog sniffing at the end of his burrow.

As the man returned to his truck, Groundhog realized what this meant. "There will be life again on this farm, but where there are farmers and dogs, there will be problems for me. I will have to move," he thought sadly.

Groundhog wouldn't have to move far, though. He knew of a perfect place up the hill, along a ridge. It was just far enough away for him to avoid trouble. He went up the ridge to look for just the right spot.

Returning, he saw the tip of Fox's tail in the distance. Groundhog moved quickly because he did not want to meet Fox out in the open. Just as Groundhog got back to his burrow, Fox came to the entrance.

"I have overheard that change is coming," declared Fox.

"Perhaps so," replied Groundhog.

"You will lose this lovely burrow. A man will never let you stay in his barn, to say nothing of a dog, which he will surely have," said Fox. Groundhog knew that this was true but said nothing.

"I have an idea that could help us both," Fox continued.

"What idea, Fox?" asked Groundhog. Now Groundhog knew that Fox had no interest in helping him. Fox had been trying to capture Groundhog for years, but still he was curious to hear what Fox had to say.

"Why don't we trade homes?" suggested Fox. "I have a cozy den up on the ridge. I admit it isn't quite as nice as this, but you could quickly dig it out further."

"Wouldn't you have problems with the man and his dog?" wondered Groundhog.

"I am a traveler, so I stay here and there, and I don't need to be in the same den every night. I would use it only now and then. Besides, I am too swift and sly for man or dog." Fox was vain, as Groundhog had always known.

Groundhog realized that Fox intended to trick him. Fox wanted to catch Groundhog away from his strong, safe burrow. Still, Groundhog did need to move, so he allowed Fox to continue.

"Why would you be willing to trade homes with me, Fox?" Groundhog inquired.

"Well, it helps both of us, really, because you have to move, and I wouldn't mind being closer to the henhouse," said Fox.

Groundhog knew that Fox was just hatching a plan to get Groundhog in a weaker burrow or to catch him out in the open as they made the trade.

"How would we switch, Fox?" asked Groundhog. "Surely, you don't think I'm just going to walk out of here in front of you."

"Well, since you can see in the dark, let's trade homes at night," suggested Fox. "I will come down the east side of the field, and you go up the west side. That way you will be perfectly safe."

Now, Groundhog knew full well that Fox could also see at night. He also realized that Fox would never keep his word.

"Fox, I agree, but with one condition. I know that you see well at night also, perhaps better than I. Let's wait until two nights from now, when the moon is full. That way I will be able to see you along the ridge line if you should happen not to keep your word," suggested Groundhog.

"You hurt my feelings," Fox smiled, "but that is a fair plan."

Fox, of course, was not going to come down the east side. He planned to come straight down the west side and catch Groundhog.

Groundhog had been thinking very carefully. The agreement to wait until the full moon would give him just the time he needed.

Meanwhile, a lot was happening on the farm. Groundhog remained in his burrow for now, even as the dog sniffed and dug around at the edge of it.

Then, on the day before the full moon, Groundhog left his burrow early in the morning before the dog was up. He carefully climbed back up onto the ridge and found Fox's home. He knew it was safe because Fox was never at home during the day. He began to dig furiously to make a nice, new safe burrow.

Sure enough, that night when the moon was full, Fox finished his hunting, and set out to find Groundhog. He trotted down the west side of the field just as Groundhog knew he would. Fox searched far into the night for Groundhog but finally realized that his plan had failed.

"Ah, well, at least there will be chickens for breakfast," Fox thought. Then he squeezed into Groundhog's old burrow and slept peacefully.

The next morning, when Fox stuck his head out, he bumped noses with the enormous dog. Fox quickly changed his mind about staying by the henhouse! Fox ran out of the barn and headed toward the ridge and his old home with the dog close on his heels. He tried to enter his old home, but Groundhog met him with sharp claws. "Sorry, Fox, this is my home now," said Groundhog. "Go back to the barn."

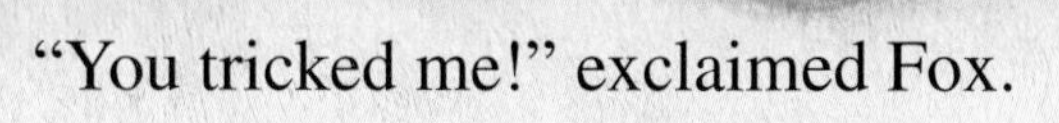

"You tricked me!" exclaimed Fox.

"Not so," said Groundhog. "We have traded homes as agreed, and even though it is true that I traded a little early, I was eager to redo this fine burrow."

"The dog knows of me now, so I can't return," said Fox.

"I'm sorry, Fox, but our trade is made," replied Groundhog.

As Fox slunk away, their neighbor, Squirrel, chattered from an oak tree.

"It seems to me," said Squirrel cheerfully, "that one who tries to trick a wise one only fools himself."

Think Critically

1. When did you realize that Groundhog would trick Fox?

2. Did Fox ever really plan to live in Groundhog's burrow in the barn? Explain your answer.

3. How does Fox help Groundhog without meaning to?

4. Tell in your own words the meaning of the sentence "One who tries to trick a wise one only fools himself."

5. What other stories come to your mind when you read this one?

Social Studies

Make a List Groundhog lives on a farm. Farms are in rural areas. Make a list of other areas where people live and what kind of home they might have in each place.

School-Home Connection Retell the story of Fox and Groundhog to family members. Then talk about other ways the story could have ended.

Word Count: 1,070